W9-BPL-007

KEEKER
and the Sugar Shack

Text © 2006 by Hadley Higginson.
Illustrations © 2006 by Maja Andersen.
All rights reserved.

Book design by Mary Beth Fiorentino.
Typeset in Weiss Medium.
The illustrations in this book were rendered in pen and ink with
digital texture.
Manufactured in China.

Library of Congress Cataloging-in-Publication Data
Higginson, Hadley.
Keeker and the sugar shack / by Hadley Higginson ; illustrated by
Maja Andersen.
p. cm.
Summary: Upon learning that an older woman has moved into
the run-down, creepy Crab Apple Hill Farm, nine-year-old Keeker
rides her pony, Plum, over to find out whether the woman is
a witch.
ISBN-13: 978-0-8118-5455-9 (library ed.)
ISBN-10: 0-8118-5455-8 (library ed.)
ISBN-13: 978-0-8118-5456-6 (pbk.)
ISBN-10: 0-8118-5456-6 (pbk.)
[1. Ponies—Fiction. 2. Neighbors—Fiction. 3. Witches—Fiction.
4. Farm life—Vermont—Fiction. 5. Vermont—Fiction.]
I. Andersen, Maja, ill. II. Title.
PZ7.H534945Kef 2006
[E]—dc22
2005027124

Distributed in Canada by Raincoast Books
9050 Shaughnessy Street, Vancouver, British Columbia V6P 6E5

10 9 8 7 6 5 4 3 2 1

Chronicle Books LLC
85 Second Street, San Francisco, California 94105

www.chroniclekids.com

KEEKER

and the Sugar Shack

by **HADLEY HIGGINSON** Illustrated by **MAJA ANDERSEN**

WITHDRAWN

North Plains Public Librar
31334 NW Commercial St
North Plains, OR 97133

chronicle books · san francisco

Chapter 1

This is Catherine Corey Keegan Dana, but everyone calls her Keeker. Keeker lives in Vermont with her mom, her dad, five dogs, two cats, a goat, a parakeet, a hamster, a goldfish—and a pony named Plum.

Keeker is almost ten. Her pony, Plum, is nearly nine. But Plum is *so* bossy. You'd think she was the older one!

Every year as the snow melts and the rain sets in, Vermont gets very muddy. So muddy, in fact, that everyone calls it mud season.

During mud season, the dirt roads get thick and gooey. Cars get stuck. Trucks get stuck. Even tractors get stuck!

It's too muddy for Keeker and Plum to go riding, so Keeker has to stay indoors a lot. It wouldn't be so bad if she had brothers·or sisters, but since she doesn't, it is SO boring. There isn't even anyone to play Yahtzee with.

Shluck-shluck-shluck—that's what it sounds like when Plum walks from one side of the field to the other.

No matter how many times Keeker suds her up and rinses her off, Plum still ends up with mud all the way up past her knees, like socks.

And every time Plum tries to dig around for some delicious grass, all she gets is . . . mud.

Plum is so bored that she's started chewing on the fence posts. Sometimes they give her lip splinters, but she doesn't care—at least it's something to do.

One Saturday after it had been raining a cold, dreary rain for what seemed like forever, the sun peeked out. Just a little.

Keeker was upstairs running around with panty hose on her head, pretending to have long braids like Laura Ingalls Wilder. Three of the dogs were wearing panty-hose hair, too.

"Mom!" yelled Keeker. "The sun is OUT! Can we go riding? Please? Please? Puh-LEEZE?"

"Well," said Mrs. Dana, "I'm not sure . . . The horses are so dirty . . ."

But with Keeker wearing panty hose on her head, it was hard to say no.

Mrs. Dana could tell that her daughter was going to lose her marbles if she had to spend even one more second inside.

"OK," said Mrs. Dana. "Go get your pony!"

"Yay!" said Keeker, and she hurried outside to catch Plum and bring her back to the barn.

"Finally!" thought Plum. Usually she tried to sneak out of going riding, but not today.

Mud season was so boring that even Plum was dying to go out.

Chapter

2

Keeker and her mom washed off Plum and Mrs. Dana's big horse, Pansy. They put on saddles and bridles, and the four of them set off down the road. *Glop-glop-glop.*

"It's like riding through peanut butter!" laughed Keeker.

"More like a nasty, marshy bog," grumped Plum as she picked her way through the muck.

Plum had never actually SEEN a nasty, marshy bog, but she imagined it would be just like this.

It took them almost an hour to get to their nearest neighbor, the Doolan Dairy. The dairy was kind of stinky (lots of cows and cow pies), but Mr. Doolan himself was very nice (and smelled good—like green grass and pipe smoke).

Normally Mr. Doolan didn't say much, but on this day he rushed out of the house, waving his arms to talk to them.

"You'll NEVER believe it," said Mr. Doolan. "Someone bought Crab Apple Hill Farm!"

Crab Apple Hill Farm was an old falling-down house with an old falling-down barn. It sat by itself up on the hill, and for as long as Keeker could remember, it had been covered in brambles and scary looking.

"Who would want to live THERE?" Keeker wondered. It gave her the creeps just thinking about it.

"Yuck, crab apples," sniffed Plum. Crab apples were small and sour and wormy. Plum preferred the fat pink apples that grew on her tree.

Keeker had a million questions.

Who bought that old farm? Had they lived there long? What were they going to do up there? Didn't they care that it was scary? Did they have kids? Or horses?

Mr. Doolan leaned in close to Keeker. "All I know," he said, "is that it's a woman, probably about your grandma's age."

All alone on that old rundown farm? "No way," thought Keeker. "Weird."

That night the rain came back. It fell and fell and fell, clattering against the windowpanes like pebbles. The wind howled.

Keeker tossed and turned under her covers. Every time she tried to close her eyes and go to sleep, all she could picture was that creepy old house up on the hill.

She tried to imagine the old lady who lived there. And in Keeker's imagination, the old lady didn't look like her grandma. She looked like . . .

A witch.

Chapter

3

The next morning the rain had stopped. It was another almost-sunshiny day, and Keeker woke up with a plan. She knew exactly what she needed to do—investigate.

"Mom," she said, in her most sugary-sweet voice, "would it be OK if I take Plum out again? Can we go by ourselves this time? Please? Please? PLEASE?"

Mrs. Dana was always a little suspicious of the sugary-sweet voice.

"Well, OK," she said, after a pause. "As long as it doesn't rain."

When Keeker got down to the barn, Plum was standing out by her water trough, sunning herself. Her eyes were closed and her whiskers were twitching—she LOVED to sunbathe.

"Mmmmmm," sighed Plum. With her eyes closed, she could imagine it was summertime and the bees were buzzing lazily around the blackberry bushes.

She was so dreamily daydreaming, in fact,
she didn't even hear Keeker come up.

Keeker brushed Plum off as fast as she could.
It wasn't easy—Plum still had most of her thick
winter coat and was as woolly as a bear.

"Why are we in such a hurry?" Plum
grumped.

Keeker was busy muttering to herself.
"There's some weird old lady up there, and no
one even CARES! . . ."

"Plum," whispered Keeker, looking both ways
to make sure no one was around, "I think that

old lady up at Crab Apple Hill Farm might be a witch. I think it's up to us to check it out."

"A witch!" thought Plum. "Hmmph." She wasn't at all sure she wanted to go someplace called Crab Apple Hill Farm. Especially since it was such a good day for sunbathing.

Then again, it did sound a bit sneaky. And Plum loved to be sneaky.

As Keeker and Plum hurried down the road, there was only one thing on their minds: How would they get up to Crab Apple Hill without being seen?

"We should go through the woods," thought Plum. It was way too early for fiddleheads, but there might be some berries left over from last summer, hiding underneath the snow.

"Yum," thought Plum.

But Keeker had a better idea.

If they cut through Mr. Doolan's cow fields, they'd come out right behind the barn at Crab Apple Hill.

"Woo-hoo!" said Keeker out loud. She was trying to pump herself up so she wouldn't be scared.

"Boo," grumped Plum. If they went that way, there would be no berries. Only cow pies.

Keeker hopped off Plum and looked around to make sure no one was watching. Then she opened the gate to the cow pasture, led Plum in, and hopped back on.

Shluck-shluck-shluck. The cow field was WAY muddier than Plum's pasture; in fact, it was downright gross. And suddenly, they were surrounded by cows.

Plum was a little nervous. She didn't like all that hot cow breath.

"Shoo!" said Keeker, waving her crop at them. She didn't seem nervous at all.

Plum huffed and puffed as they climbed the hill. The cows didn't seem to mind. They mooed and bobbed their heads as Plum and Keeker trudged by.

Finally, they got to the top. And there, standing right in front of the path into the woods, was . . .

A bull. A big, mean-looking bull with a ring in his nose and everything.

Chapter

4

Keeker took a big deep breath. Her heart was whumping, and her mind was racing. What should she do? How would they get by that big old bull?

This had happened to her and her mom before when they'd been out riding, and her mom always just calmly rode around the bulls.

"OK, Plum," said Keeker. "Just ignore him. He won't bother us if we don't bother him."

They made a WIDE circle around the bull and hurried into the woods.

"Phew!" said Keeker. She was so relieved she felt as if she might faint.

"Dumb old bull," thought Plum. Now that they were past him, he didn't seem so scary.

They went just a little way, until they hit a falling-down stone wall. On the other side of the wall was the messiest, muddiest barnyard Keeker had ever seen.

Crab Apple Hill Farm.

"Surely only a witch would live here," Keeker thought. She could just imagine all the spells and potions bubbling away.

Keeker climbed off Plum and hunkered down behind the stone wall. She tugged on the reins to see if she could get Plum to hunker, too.

"Ponies don't bend like that," snorted Plum.

So instead, Keeker tried a disguise. She picked some branches and tucked them into Plum's bridle.

From where they were hunkering, Keeker
and Plum could clearly see the house, the barn
and, off to the side, a little falling-down shack.
The shack had a chimney with smoke coming
out of it. It had little tiny windows. It was too
small to be a house and way too small to be
a barn.

"Aha!" thought Keeker. There must be a cauldron in there, cooking over a fire. She thought
of some especially creepy witches she'd seen in
a play. "Bubble, bubble, toil and trouble . . ."

Suddenly—*scrrrrrreeeeeeeeeekkkk*—the screen
door at the back of the house swung open, and
an old lady came out carrying a kettle.

She had wild gray hair and was wearing a
kooky skirt and a couple of coats. A big hairy
dog snuffled along behind her.

Laughing and cackling, the old lady walked
right by where Keeker and Plum were hiding
and disappeared into the shack.

Keeker's heart started whumping again. Even Plum couldn't quite believe her eyes.

"She's totally a witch," whispered Keeker. "I've never seen anyone who looked so kooky! And did you see that dog? It was huge! I think it might have been . . . a woof!"

(Keeker had trouble saying her *l*s. She meant "a wolf.")

The old lady stayed in the shack for what seemed like forever. Keeker's knees were wet, and her back hurt from hunkering.

Plum was uncomfortable, too—the branches in her bridle were starting to feel very poky. And even though she didn't like to admit it, she was very afraid of wolves.

Keeker began to think of all the scary stories she'd read, stories about kids alone in the woods with witches. What was that old lady DOING in there? What exactly was in that cauldron?

"Yikes," said Keeker softly to herself. Now she was really scared.

Even Plum started to shiver a little bit.

Just then—*scrrrrrreeeeeeeeeekkkk*—the crooked door on the shack swung open, and the old lady came out again, with the big dog right behind her.

She hurried past Plum and Keeker, humming to herself. But the big dog did NOT hurry past. In fact, it stopped right in front of Keeker and Plum.

"Oh, no," thought Keeker miserably. But it was too late. The big hairy dog was climbing over the falling-down wall and coming right for them.

"HELP!" Keeker shrieked, "WOOF! RUN!"

She grabbed Plum's reins and scrambled over the wall, with Plum scrambling right behind her.

They sprinted across the barnyard with the huge woof panting behind them.

Chapter

5

Keeker had no choice but to dash inside the house, sliding on a rug and almost tumbling into the coat closet. Plum went clattering into the chicken coop, sending feathers flying (and making all the chickens flap and squawk).

The huge woof-dog skidded to a stop and began to lick its paws.

Inside the house, Keeker burst into the kitchen—and got the surprise of her life.

There, sitting at a little yellow table, was her mom. Eating pancakes.

"Keeker!" coughed Mrs. Dana, startled. "What on EARTH are you doing here?"

"Mom!" panted Keeker, "What are YOU doing here! Why are you eating PANCAKES at the WITCH HOUSE?"

Mrs. Dana just laughed. "Oh, Keeker. Honestly!"

"What's this about a witch?" said the old lady, coming through the kitchen door.

Up close, she didn't look very scary. Her kooky skirt had big flowers all over it, and she had pink cheeks and twinkly eyes.

"Ummm, Keeker, this is our new neighbor, Mavis Yardbottom," said Keeker's mom. "She's been making maple syrup, and she invited me over to taste the first batch."

"Pancakes, hon?" asked Mavis Yardbottom, bending over Keeker with a big stack of flapjacks.

Keeker felt very, very, very silly. Especially since the pancakes were delicious, and Mavis was as nice as she could be.

After they'd all had seconds and thirds (and rescued Plum from the henhouse), Mavis took them out to see the sugar shack.

"This is where the magic happens!" Mavis said happily. "This is where I boil the tree sap to make the maple syrup."

There was absolutely nothing scary in the sugar shack. Just vats of sap, bubbling away and turning into sweet-smelling syrup.

Since Plum hadn't gotten any pancakes, Mavis gave her a maple-sugar candy, which was just as good. The big dog got one, too.

"His name is Clancy," said Mavis, patting him on his hairy head. "Isn't he a sweetie?"

He was sweet. He didn't even mind when Plum nosed over and ate his candy, too.

That night it rained again. But it wasn't a cold, clattering kind of rain; it was more gentle. *Ping-ping-ping.*

Plum curled up in her stall, licking her lips. For once, there was no mud in her whiskers— just maple sugar. Keeker fell asleep with her hands still syrup-sticky. (As usual, she had only pretended to wash her hands before dinner.)

Up on the hill, the old falling-down house didn't look so scary anymore. Lamplight glowed in the windows. Mavis Yardbottom was tucked in under her favorite quilt, and next to her bed the big hairy dog snuffled and snored.

Smoke from the sugar shack spun up into the sky, blanketing the woods like cotton candy. Everyone slept soundly (and everyone's dreams were extra sweet).

GALLOPING YOUR WAY IN SPRING 2007

Introducing a new adventure in the Sneaky Pony series

KEEKER
and the Springtime Surprise

It's springtime in Vermont, and Keeker and Plum have discovered all kinds of surprising things on the farm. Keeker finds a baby bird on the lawn. Plum has a new family of groundhogs living in her field. And Keeker's parents are acting very, very mysterious. They're spending an awful lot of time in the barn with Keeker's mom's horse, Pansy. What's going on? Determined not to be ignored, Keeker and Plum decide to stage a major theatrical event. But as the play ends, the plot takes a surprising twist that they never could have imagined!

North Plains Public Library
31334 NW Commercial St.
North Plains, OR 97133